THE SHADOW CHILDREN

D1410958

The Shadow Children

BY STEVEN SCHNUR

ILLUSTRATED BY HERBERT TAUSS

SCHOLASTIC INC.

NEW YORK TORONTO LONDON AUCKLAND SYDNEY

ISBN 0-590-93429-5

Text copyright © 1994 by Steven Schnur.
Illustrations copyright © 1994 by Herbert Tauss.
All rights reserved. Published by Scholastic Inc., 555 Broadway, New York, NY 10012, by arrangement with William Morrow and Company, Inc.

12 11 10 9 8 7 6 5 4 3 2 1   6 7 8 9/9 0 1/0

Printed in the U.S.A.   23

First Scholastic printing, October 1996

In loving memory of
Moise Amariglio
—S. S.

In memory of my parents and
my brother Martin
—H. T.

*All the things one has forgotten
cry out for help in dreams.*
—ELIAS CANETTI

CHAPTER
One

My grandfather lived all his life on a small farm in the high country near the village of Mont Brulant. I spent my summers there as a boy, learning to ride and swim and cast for trout in the icy mountain streams, and to plow a straight furrow through the dark, volcanic soil. It was the place I loved most in all the world, a place full of unfamiliar freedoms and unexpected discoveries. In my earliest years, just after the Second World War, my parents accompanied me on the long trip out to the farm and left me there in the care of my grandparents, retrieving me again just before school resumed in the fall. But the year I turned eleven they let me make the journey alone. My grandmother had died that winter and Mama worried that Grandfather might be lonely. So, the first day of vacation I boarded the train carrying a heavy suitcase, a return ticket, and instructions to "take special care of Grand-père."

I was not the only one traveling alone that day. The train was crowded with children put on at one end by parents and taken off

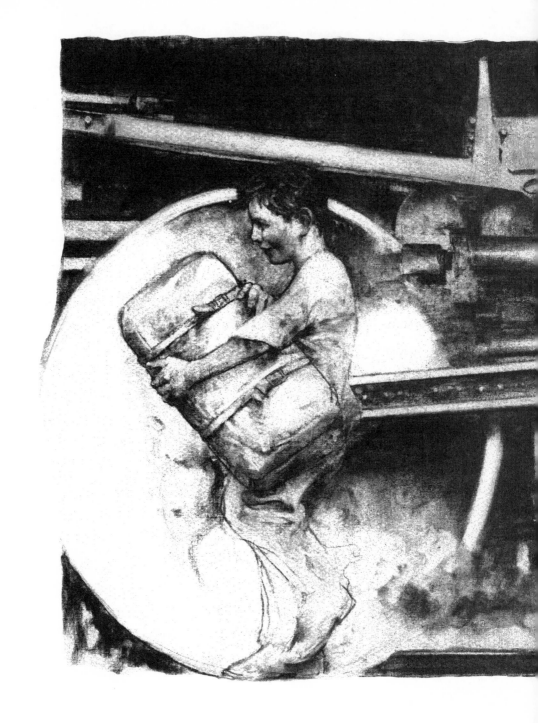

at the other by grandparents, or aunts and uncles. The conductor, a heavy, red-faced man with a thick black mustache and a large pocket watch, helped us find seats and made sure we got off at our stops. During the long hours in between we ate the hard-boiled eggs and sausages our mothers had packed, our feet tapping to the rhythmic clatter of the rails, our faces pressed to the windows, watching the scenery change from tall buildings and crowded city streets to open fields and endless green forests. As it did I felt my chest expand, imagining I was no longer just a boy on vacation but a young man leaving home to make my way in the world. I didn't know then that my summer alone with Grand-père would, in fact, mark the end of my childhood.

He was waiting for me as the train pulled into the tiny depot at Mont Brulant, scattering chickens and sleeping dogs. I spotted him sitting on the high wooden seat of his wagon, squinting into the afternoon sun, the smoke from his pipe curling around his white head. "Grand-père!" I shouted, sliding open the compartment window and waving. He smiled, knocked the pipe against his shoe, and began to climb down. His great white mare, Reveuse, the dreamer, stood nearly motionless in the heat, her long, uncombed tail switching listlessly at flies. There was no larger horse in all the world, it seemed to me, and none slower. I was so happy to see them both that I laughed.

As Grand-père approached the train the conductor pulled my

suitcase from the rack above the seat and handed it down through the window, then tossed a large canvas sack after it, shouting, "You're a popular man this week, Monsieur Hoirie." I bounded down the steps and into Grand-père's arms. He took my head in his rough hands and kissed my cheeks, his gray eyes shining. Then to the conductor he called proudly, "My grandson," placing his hand on my head.

"Fine boy," the conductor said, scanning the platform for late arrivals. "He'll make a good farmer, just like his grandfather?"

"For the summer, at least," Grand-père replied.

The conductor smiled, blew his whistle, checked the platform one last time, then waved the engineer on. A moment later the great black train jerked forward, pulling slowly away from the station.

"You've grown," Grand-père said, taking me by the shoulders. The sweet aroma of his pipe, of molasses, curing hay, and burning leaves—the scent of the farm itself—filled the air. "Soon you'll be too big to spend summers with your cranky old grandfather, won't you? But not just yet."

"Not ever." I smiled, blinking in the bright blue light that made Mont Brulant shimmer like no other place I knew.

He clapped me on both shoulders, then limped back to the wagon carrying the heavy sack in one hand and my suitcase in the other. Reveuse neighed as I approached, dropping her head to be stroked. "She doesn't forget," Grand-père said, handing me two large sugar cubes. Reveuse ate them from my open palm, tickling my hand with her rough, wet lips.

"Did they take good care of you on the train?" he asked. I nodded, stroking Reveuse, her smooth white coat rippling loosely beneath my fingers. "You must be hungry after such a long ride," he added, lifting my suitcase and the dirty gray sack into the wagon.

"Starving," I replied. He rumpled my hair and laughed. "When *isn't* an eleven-year-old boy hungry? Come, we've got a long way to go." With a boost from his powerful arms, I leapt up to the high seat and looked out over the village square.

Beneath the linden trees a dozen old men sat watching a game of *boule,* shouting encouragement as the heavy metal balls rolled through the dust and clanged against each other. Monsieur Jaboter, the butcher, stood cleaving meat in the window of his shop. The aroma of sheep and fresh-baked bread drifted across the cobblestone square, followed closely by the pungent smell of cheese. It was all so familiar, and yet somehow different. Something had changed. The town looked smaller than I remembered, emptier. What had become of the grand sparkling fountain and the large red-tiled houses facing the depot? In their place stood a handful of small shops and a trickling spout used to water the horses. Even the old men seemed smaller. Grand-père too.

For just a moment I felt a pang of disappointment, but then Grand-père climbed up beside me, clicked his tongue, and cooed,

"Home, my lady," and slowly Reveuse came to life, yanking the heavy, groaning wagon forward, clopping loudly across the cobblestones, that hollow, happy sound restoring my delight in the place. A few of the old men nodded as we passed. Monsieur Jaboter leaned out his door and called, "How long will you have the boy?"

"Long enough to empty your shop," Grand-père called back. The men in the square laughed; Monsieur Jaboter smiled and bowed. A moment later the tiny village was behind us. When I looked back, it was nothing more than a knot of red roofs surrounded by green hills and neatly plowed fields. Before us orchards, pastures, and pine forests rose and fell in gentle waves to the horizon. My skin tingled at the vastness of it. I wanted to leap down from the wagon and climb the haystacks, run along the stone walls, ride the grazing horses. I couldn't believe my good fortune: two whole months of vacation alone with Grand-père, two months to fish every stream, swim every pond, and climb every hill in Mont Brulant.

"Not bad, eh?" Grand-père said, sensing my excitement. "This is where a boy belongs, not on those crowded city streets of yours."

Reveuse followed the railroad tracks for several miles, then turned off onto a narrow lane lined with chestnut trees that cast long shadows in the late afternoon light. Spotted cows lolled in the shade, raising their heads as we rattled by. The warm air smelled of wild roses and cow dung. I breathed deeply and smiled. It was more beautiful than I had remembered. Grand-père took a pear from the wide pocket of his blue smock, shined it on his forearm, and handed it to me. "The last one," he said. "It waited all winter for you." As I bit into it the sweet juice ran down my chin. "Like a true peasant," he laughed, watching me wipe it away with the back of my hand. Then he pulled me close and kissed the top of my head.

Like most of his neighbors, Grand-père was a farmer. Every summer he raised a small crop of wheat, alfalfa, and corn. In the fall he harvested the pears from his hillside orchard. Once a week Madame Jaboter, the butcher's wife, rode out to the farm to do Grand-père's laundry and help with the housecleaning. Saturdays he rode into town to collect his mail, attend to errands, and sit a few hours with his neighbors in the shade of the linden trees. The rest of the week he spent alone with only Reveuse and the chickens for company.

After Grand-mère died, Mama urged him to sell the farm and move in with us, but he said he could never leave Mont Brulant, not after sixty years. "A man my age can't be transplanted," he explained. "I'd shrivel up and blow away like an old leaf." Knowing how frugal he was, Mama tried to convince him that our living together would be more economical, but he only laughed. "Who'd buy this old place?" he asked. "No one wants to live in Mont Brulant anymore. Look at you." Like so many other farm children, Mama had moved to the city as soon as she was old enough to leave

home. "Don't worry about me," Grand-père assured her. "I've no time to be lonely. There's too much to do."

And there was, for in addition to planting crops, raising chickens, harvesting pears, and tending the small vegetable garden beyond the kitchen, Grand-père was also a bookbinder. Once a month the train delivered a sack of broken books that Grand-père patiently repaired for a bookseller in the city, performing small miracles where others had given up hope. Whenever he wasn't tending to farm chores, he sat at his workbench in the narrow shed beside the barn, carefully sewing loose pages together and binding them between sturdy boards. He would strip away the old, crumbling covers, trim the frayed pages, then painstakingly rebuild the decaying books until they were unrecognizable in gleaming new bindings, their titles hand stamped in the little press he sometimes let me operate. I was amazed that his thick, calloused fingers could perform such delicate work. Nothing, not even an abundant harvest, seemed to give him as much pleasure as a single book beautifully bound.

As Reveuse plodded slowly toward Grand-père's farm, kicking up clouds of dust, we passed four ragged children walking by the side of the road. The oldest, a tall, skinny girl about my age, with deep-set eyes and matted black hair, clutched a baby awkwardly to her chest. Her shapeless dress fell off one shoulder, hanging almost to

her shoes. Behind her walked two barefoot boys in tattered shorts. They could have been twins.

In the years just after the war I often saw such children wandering from town to town, though never near Mont Brulant. Mama called them refugees, children without homes. We would stop to offer them something to eat or a little money, their dark, pleading eyes always so full of hunger. They gulped down the bread and cheese we provided without pausing to taste it, then begged for more, clinging to our sleeves until we shook ourselves free and rode on, leaving them beside the road with empty, outstretched hands. Some of them had blue numbers tattooed across their forearms.

I always felt ashamed after those confrontations: I had so much—a closet full of clothes, three meals a day, a warm bed, my parents—while they had nothing, not even hope. Sometimes I dreamt I was being chased up a ladder by those hungry eyes. Strange hands clutched at my ankles, trying to pull me down toward a blazing fire. I awoke screaming, my nightshirt damp with sweat.

As we neared the four children Reveuse slowed, expecting as I did that Grand-père would stop and offer them something: a few coins, some bread, a drink of water. But instead he clicked his tongue and urged her on, passing the children as though he hadn't seen them. The tall girl extended her hand, palm up, almost touching me, her fathomless black eyes pleading for food. I shuddered.

She had the eyes of my dream. "Grand-père, they look so hungry," I said, turning to him. He studied me a moment, the sunlight reflecting in his gray eyes, then asked with a grin, "The cows?"

"The children!" I cried, pointing. But when I turned back they were gone.

I forgot all about the refugees in my excitement upon reaching the farm. A cloud of squawking chickens and honking geese welcomed us, scurrying across the barnyard as we pulled up to the old stone house. Grand-père carried my suitcase up the steep stairs to his bedroom, pausing midway to catch his breath. He now slept on the sitting room couch beside the fireplace. "At my age a man begins to count his steps," he explained, dropping my suitcase on the bed. He pointed to the basin of water by the window, handed me a towel and soap, then returned to the kitchen to prepare dinner. I washed the dust from my face and hands looking out over green fields already knee-high in wheat. Long ago Mama had made a pencil sketch of that view and hung it over my bed at home. Now it came to life in all its glittering vibrancy: hens scuttering this way and that, Reveuse chewing loudly on carrots, Grand-père pumping water from the well, blue jays and bright red cardinals darting among the shadowy pear trees. Far in the distance the mountain for which Mont Brulant was named shimmered in the waning orange sunlight, its wildflower meadows glowing faintly red as though on fire.

When I came downstairs, the kitchen table was already set with bread and cheese, two silver candlesticks, and a large bowl of fruit. Grand-père stood before the stove, a white apron tied around his thick waist. "A poor imitation of your grand-mère's stew, God rest her soul," he said, ladling out thick chunks of lamb, "but we won't starve. Sit." He carried two steaming plates to the table, removed his apron, raised his wineglass, and said, *"Bon appétit, mon cher."* Then he broke off two large hunks of bread, handed me one, pointed to my plate, and said, "And now our summer begins. Eat."

Two

I awoke the next morning to crowing roosters and the rattling of pots and pans. Grand-père was talking to the chickens and geese as he tossed bits of stale bread out the kitchen door. The aroma of freshly baked rolls filled the house. The sun was already above the trees. I hurried outside to wash beneath the pump, threading my way carefully through all the animals, then took my place at the knotty pine table in the kitchen, its surface as etched with age as Grand-père's weathered face.

"Did you sleep well?" he asked, cracking eggs into a heavy iron skillet. They began to sizzle the moment they hit the pan.

"I dreamt of those refugees," I said, picturing the four children still trudging through the dust.

"What refugees?" Grand-père asked.

"The ones we passed yesterday."

"On the train?"

"On our way here from Mont Brulant."

"You must have dozed off," he said, setting a heavy brown crock of fresh butter on the table. "There aren't any refugees here—except for city ones like you." He filled half my cup with coffee, then added warm milk from the stove. "And what were these refugees doing in your dream?"

"Eating pears," I said, leaning over to sip my café au lait. It tasted much sweeter and richer than the coffee we drank at home.

"Then they weren't refugees but gypsies!" Grand-père declared with sudden annoyance. "Turn your back for one minute and they'll steal you blind. Late at night I hear them in the orchard, stripping the branches bare. They're worse than crows. Next time I'll take my horsewhip to them."

"They were just hungry," I said, surprised by his vehemence.

"If they have their way, we'll be the hungry ones."

After breakfast I swept out the kitchen and fireplace while Grand-père washed the dishes. Before the sun became too strong, I weeded the vegetable garden, then brushed Reveuse in her stall, collected eggs from the henhouse, and helped Grand-père hammer pear crates together from strips of old barn siding. We ate lunch in the shade of the orchard, sharing bread and cheese and a small bottle of red wine, which Grand-père poured sparingly into my cup of water. Then we lay back in the unmowed grass, watching thin white clouds through the almond-shaped leaves, the high-pitched call of cardinals piercing the still air.

The rest of that day I spent riding Reveuse around the farm, rediscovering my favorite haunts—the green cow pond full of bullfrogs, the hollow ash where I used to hide acorns and carefully polished chestnuts, and the iron gate in the farthest corner of the pasture that led nowhere. Reveuse was huge, almost seven feet tall, and, like Grand-père, gentle and slow-moving. I never saw her trot or gallop; she was a walker, a plodder. From the safety of her high back I could see out over miles of countryside.

The first week of vacation I stayed close to Grand-père, helping to turn and stack the hay, gather honey from the hives, mow the grass between the pear trees, and even pull waxed white threads through the pages of old, damaged books. At the end of those long days, weak with hunger, I collapsed on the sofa and napped until dinner, my arms and legs aching, the back of my neck sunburnt. After the dishes had been washed and put away I lay before the fireplace poking at the small blaze Grand-père kindled on all but the warmest nights. "When you get to be my age," he explained, patting his chest, "the furnace in here doesn't heat so well."

Whenever it got too hot for me indoors, I sat by the pump in the barnyard listening to bullfrogs and searching the sky for shooting stars. Sometimes they fell one at a time, just brief flashes of light that vanished the moment I spotted them; other times they hurtled across the black night in great white showers. Once, when the sky seemed to light up with long streaks of stars, I cried, "Grand-père, come see!" But by the time he limped to the doorway the cascade had ended.

"Your grand-mère loved them too," he said, sounding unusually tired and lonely that night. "She used to sit there for hours, just like you, her head bent back." He studied the sky a moment, then returned to the couch. He often fell asleep with an open book across his chest, his reading glasses perched on the tip of his nose. I would carefully remove the glasses and book, blow out the lamp beside the sofa, shut the back door, then tiptoe up the creaking stairs to bed, drifting off to sleep surrounded by the sounds of crickets and frogs and the occasional neighing of Reveuse.

That first Thursday morning Madame Jaboter knocked on the kitchen door as Grand-père and I were finishing up breakfast. She was a short barrel-shaped woman with bright red hair gathered in a thick knot on the top of her round head. Her plump face and figure reminded me of those hollow dolls that fit one inside the other. Every summer she pretended not to recognize me.

"Excuse me, Monsieur Hoirie," she said, pausing in the doorway. "I didn't realize you had company. I'll come back later."

"Come in, silly woman," he said, laughing, "and say hello to Etienne."

"Etienne?" she replied, covering her mouth with both hands. *"Mais non,* it's not possible, not my *petit* Etienne! This is some grown-up impostor."

"It's me!" I smiled, rising. "Honest."

She stepped back as if startled, squinting at me in disbelief. "That's not the voice of my Etienne. It's much too deep."

Grand-père laughed. "What's one to do with such a woman?"

"Wait, this will decide," she said, pulling a small brown parcel from her apron. "My Etienne could tell me what I'm holding."

"Spiced sausage." I smiled.

Her arms burst open. "It *is* my Etienne," she declared, hugging me. Her apron smelled of lilac water and garlic. "And do you still love Monsieur Jaboter's meat sticks?"

"I missed them all winter," I told her.

"And not Madame Jaboter?" she frowned.

"Of course, you too," I quickly added.

"One would never know. Not a single letter all these months. Every week I ask Monsieur Hoirie, 'Is Etienne sick? He promised to write.' Other boys might forget but not my Etienne, not unless he isn't feeling well."

"I did have a bad cold," I said.

"Then you are forgiven." She smiled, releasing me. "But not before you do absolution." Then without pausing for answers she asked in rapid succession, "Tell me about your dear *maman,* and how did you do in school this term, and have you taken a girlfriend yet"—I wrinkled my nose and shook my head—"and what have you decided to be now that you are almost grown? *Vite,* quick! I want to know everything."

I spent the next hour sitting on a stool beside the stove chewing sausage sticks and answering her questions while she scrubbed our laundry in Grand-mère's old tin washtub. "It's good you're here," she said, loud enough for Grand-père to hear in the bindery. "He's been very lonely since your poor grand-mère…" Out of concern for my feelings she did not finish the sentence. "Have you noticed how thin he's become? I'm forever reminding him to eat. How would Monsieur Jaboter survive if all his customers ate like penitent monks?"

She wiped the suds from her thick red forearms and smoothed the stray hairs about her ears. "Our little village is getting too old. Even your dear Madame Jaboter is not so young anymore. But you'll help put the spring back into our step."

That afternoon I rode beyond the borders of the farm for the first time, plodding down a narrow lane between abandoned fields thick with brambles and birch saplings. The farther I got from Grand-père's farm the more deserted the landscape became, open fields gradually giving way to dark woods, farmhouses and barns disappearing altogether.

I kept to the lane until we reached the pine forest at the foot of Mont Brulant. There I turned off onto what appeared to be an abandoned road in the middle of the trees. It was wide enough for two wagons to pass and as straight and level as a railroad track but showed no sign of use. The trees closed in overhead, blocking out the light. Something in the utter stillness of the place chilled me. It seemed to bother Reveuse too, for she walked reluctantly over the thick bed of pine needles, snorting nervously, frequently hesitating, then stopping altogether, refusing to cross an old stone bridge about a mile into the woods.

"What's the matter?" I asked, dismounting and attempting to lead her over it on foot. "Is it the bridge?" I studied it a moment, then walked across and back to show her it was sturdy enough to support us. "See. It won't collapse. It's stone." But she wasn't listening. Her large black eyes darted from side to side, full of terror. Suddenly the skin on my arms bristled. "Is it wolves?" I whispered, returning to the safety of her back. "Where are they? Show me." But her head just twisted from side to side as though she were trying to throw off her bridle. And then I heard it, a low moan like a sobbing child or the distant whistle of a train. "Shh!" I said, sitting very still in the saddle, tightly clutching the reins. "Is that it, that crying sound?" Reveuse backed nervously, as if in answer.

"Is someone there?" I called weakly. High overhead the trees rustled sharply, but only a faint whisper of wind penetrated the woods below. Then Reveuse began to snort and whinny, backing down from the level clearing into the undergrowth. "Reveuse!" I shouted, kicking her ribs, but she kept on backing and snorting. The wind grew stronger, the moaning louder, and then suddenly she reared up, throwing me from the saddle. I thought she was going to bolt, leaving me to face the invisible terror alone. But just

as suddenly she grew calm. The treetops stopped swaying, the whispering vanished. I brushed myself off and took hold of her harness but could not coax her back up to the clearing. So finally I led her out of the forest through the underbrush and headed back to the farm.

When I told Grand-père about the old road I'd discovered he explained that it wasn't a road at all but an abandoned spur of the main railroad. Long ago tracks had run through that part of the forest in the shadow of Mont Brulant but had been pulled up during the war. All that remained was a wide path through the trees and two or three crumbling stone viaducts, bridges to nowhere.

"What do you think frightened Reveuse?" I asked.

"She was probably just tired," he ruminated. "She's not that young anymore. You rode a long way."

"But she threw me."

"Reveuse! I can't believe that. You must have dozed off." He squeezed my shoulder. "The summer sun makes us all sleepy."

"But I was wide-awake, I swear."

"Then perhaps Reveuse dozed off," he laughed. "Horses have bad dreams too. That's why we call them night*mares*!" He pinched my nose and winked, but I didn't return his smile. I was annoyed with him for not taking me seriously.

When Madame Jaboter returned the following Thursday I told her what had happened in the woods. She didn't laugh.

Instead she took hold of my wrist and whispered gravely, "Promise me you won't go back there."

I thought she was joking. "Why not?" I asked.

"Promise me!" she repeated even more fervently.

"Why should I?"

"It's not safe," she replied, deadly earnest. "Those woods are haunted."

I laughed in nervous recognition of my own momentary fear.

"Etienne, I mean it. You mustn't," she insisted, dropping her voice and looking over my shoulder. "The souls of a thousand lost children live in those woods."

"Ghosts?" I asked, still smiling.

"Yes, ghosts," she whispered sharply.

"I'm too old to believe in that."

"Then call them memories."

"What do you mean?" I asked.

"I can't explain. Just promise." Her small brown eyes bore into me.

"Grand-père knows I go there," I replied, trying to assume an indifferent air despite the tingling sensation at the back of my neck. "He doesn't mind."

"We don't like to speak of it."

"Of what?" I asked impatiently.

"I told you, I can't explain, I only know what I know. Don't go back. Please, Etienne."

"I'm not afraid," I insisted, and ran out of the kitchen. But I was. So that evening, as Grand-père and I rode back from town after leaving Madame Jaboter at her husband's shop, I asked him what she meant by "the souls of a thousand lost children."

"Just a lot of superstitious nonsense," he snapped with unexpected anger, glancing back over his shoulder. "Ignore her when she speaks that way."

"But she seemed so worried," I said, beginning to sense that he was hiding something from me.

"Bah. She'll worry herself to death with old wives' tales."

"You don't mind if I go back there?"

"Of course not. I've fished beneath that bridge more times than I can count. And I'm still here." He pounded his chest and smiled. "Don't listen to her prattle. She's just a foolish old woman."

Then why did her words make him so angry? I wondered. And what had spooked Reveuse? And who were those lost children Madame Jaboter referred to? Where did they come from? There were no children in Mont Brulant. Everyone was old: the townspeople, the farmers, even the horses. As we waved to the same old men sitting around the village square I realized I hadn't seen a single child in town all summer, except for the four we passed coming from the train.

"Why aren't there any young people here?" I asked.

Grand-père shrugged. "Ever since the war they all want to live in the city. They leave as soon as they finish school, just like your mother. Mont Brulant's too quiet, they say, too slow, too set in its ways. But without young couples there can't be any change and there certainly can't be any children. Every year we get a little older, a little frailer. Too many farmhouses sit empty, too many fields lie choked with weeds. After we're gone, who'll keep the farms? One day it'll all be forest again, no more Mont Brulant."

CHAPTER

Three

*E*very other Thursday, after driving Madame Jaboter back to town, Grand-père and I stopped at the train depot to drop off the books he had repaired. He was quieter than usual on those trips, parting with his handiwork reluctantly, almost mournfully. Whenever he prepared the books for shipment, carefully wrapping them in thick layers of old newspaper, he grew thoughtful, turning them over in his hands, running his fingers along the spines, reading a few last paragraphs.

"They're like my children," he once explained. "It's hard to send them out into the world to be neglected and abused. I'll miss them."

But one long row of books was never returned. Summer after summer they remained on the same high shelf to the left of the fireplace. Larger and more elegant than the others, they were bound not in cloth but brown leather and stamped with gold letters in a language I could not read. Even Grand-père did not understand the words.

"If you can't read them, why keep them?" I asked one evening, lying before the fire.

"They don't belong to me," he replied, following my eyes to the high shelf. "A young man left them here for safekeeping long ago and promised to return for them."

"What happened to him?" I asked.

"I don't know," Grand-père answered vacantly.

"Did you repair them?"

"You should have seen them," he said, rising with difficulty from his chair. "In tatters, covers missing, pages torn, water-stained. I took great pains with these." He wiped his hands on his pants and removed one. "Smell." He held the book to my nose. It reminded me of a well-oiled saddle. Then he opened it. The large pages were crammed with odd-shaped letters.

"What's it say?" I asked.

He shrugged. "No idea."

"How long have you had them?"

"Since the war."

"Maybe the owner just forgot about them," I suggested.

"You don't forget about books like these," Grand-père reflected.

"Then maybe he died."

"Maybe," he echoed thoughtfully, placing the book back on the shelf.

•   •   •   •   •

Several days later the weather turned so hot that all heavy work on the farm ceased. The long, blistering days echoed with the deafening vibrations of crickets, the warm nights with distant heat lightning and occasional violent thunderstorms. After dinner, instead of reading by the fireplace, Grand-père sat in the barnyard fanning himself with discarded book covers, his feet in a bucket of cold water. Mornings he sought the shade of the bindery while I rode off to fish below the old stone bridge. The heat was especially hard on Reveuse. She lumbered along more slowly than usual, head down, stopping at every tiny rivulet to drink until we reached the old railroad spur. Then, as before, she became skittish, refusing to cross the bridge. So I tied her up and walked on alone, shadowed by an eerie tingling sensation, as though I were being watched. Even on the hottest days it remained strangely cool among the pines. The shaded hollows held pockets of air so cold they made me shiver; the river numbed my feet.

On one of those mornings I left Reveuse at the bridge and continued on through the trees, propelled by a growing curiosity. How could an entire railroad have disappeared without a trace? I walked along the track bed, kicking absentmindedly through the thick layer of orange pine needles. I had not walked far when my foot unearthed something that sparkled in the warm white light. I reached down and discovered a small gold bracelet just large enough for an infant's tiny wrist. From it dangled a single pendant heart with letters engraved upon it that reminded me of the large books beside the fireplace. That night I showed it to Grand-père.

"Pretty," he said, barely glancing at it.

"Who do you think it belongs to?" I asked, polishing the little heart with a corner of my napkin. It shone brightly in the candle-light.

"To you now," he answered curtly.

"But how'd it get there?"

"The woods are full of such things," he said with a shade of annoyance. The heat had made him as cranky as Reveuse. "On Sundays people like to walk there. It's cool. They picnic. Children drop things." He stared down at his plate as he spoke, then finished the meal in silence. Only later, as I lay in the orchard, looking up at the stars, did I think to ask, "What children?" But by then he had fallen asleep.

When I came down for breakfast the next morning, Grand-père had a sour expression on his face. He grunted in response to my *bonjour,* then disappeared inside the bindery, leaving me to eat alone. I thought he was angry because I'd spent so much time away from the farm, so all that morning I tended to chores, then stood in the doorway of the bindery watching him work. He seemed unaware of me, muttering occasionally to himself as he wiped the sweat from his forehead and neck. He looked suddenly older, smaller, more bent with age, the hair on the top of his head so thin I could see his spotted brown scalp through it. Then he accidental-

ly pricked his finger and cursed loudly. Looking up, he stared at me a moment in surprise, shook out his injured hand, and declared, "Too hot, *mon cher.* Why don't you go for a swim."

"Come with me," I pleaded.

"With this leg?" he replied, patting his right hip. "I would drown."

I rarely thought about Grand-père's limp, since he all but ignored it himself, climbing into pear trees, plowing fields, even retiling roofs. It seemed less a handicap than a habit, like the way he grasped a knife, slicing sausage and cheese toward his thumb. I thought of it as nothing more than his heavily accented way of walking.

"Did you always limp?" I asked.

"Since the war," he replied, squeezing his injured finger.

"I didn't know you were in the army."

"It's not that noble a wound." He snorted. "I was too old to fight."

I waited for him to explain. Finally he said, "Reveuse kicked me." He pointed just below his right hip. "Almost lost the leg."

"Reveuse?" I cried in astonishment.

"She was not always the great lady she is today," he explained. "Once upon a time she was so full of energy she could have pulled a plow straight to the summit of Mont Brulant."

I knew that from being thrown off her back. "But why'd she kick you?"

"Who knows? Maybe she didn't feel like being harnessed that day. Even animals have their moods. Go, take your swim. It's too hot to talk." He picked up the needle and resumed sewing. I watched him another moment, wondering if it was really just the heat that made him so grumpy or something I had done.

"You sure I can't help?" I asked.

"Go," he said, shaking his head without looking up. So I saddled Reveuse and rode toward Mont Brulant, which quivered in the noon sun like an ancient volcano.

"Did you really break Grand-père's leg?" I asked, leaning forward against her neck. She trudged along head down, searching for water. In the distance, the dirt lane glistened as if wet. Halfway to the mountain I thought I spotted a distant wagon approaching, but as we came over the next rise the road was empty. My eyes stung from the glare and dust; my head throbbed. "Come on, Reveuse." I prodded her ribs, eager to reach the shade, but she ignored both my voice and my heels.

When, finally, we entered the shade of the forest, I tied her beside a stream and continued on foot, searching the ground for more treasure, relieved by the sharp cold air that swirled like fog about the pine needles. The woods were oddly silent, no crickets or honeybees, not even the rustle of foraging squirrels or the snap of crows' wings. Nothing moved.

But as I neared the bridge I thought I heard voices. I stopped and turned my head. Nothing. Sliding my feet through the pine needles, I moved forward slowly, silently, listening carefully, holding my breath. And then it returned, just a murmur, barely distinguishable from the gurgling river. Grand-père was right, I thought, children *were* picnicking in the woods.

I hurried to the bridge and peered down into the tumbling water below. Somewhere children were chanting, reciting a lesson, but I couldn't see them or understand their words.

"Hello?" I called. "Where are you?" The chanting stopped. I turned my ear toward the river. Someone was whispering, or was it just water cascading over stones? Then something stirred in the shadow of the stone arch. I shuddered, afraid to move, hearing Madame Jaboter's warning in my ear: "It's not safe. Those woods are haunted." From beneath the bridge stepped a young man with a wispy brown beard and round rimless glasses. He held a large tattered book in one hand, a half-eaten pear in the other. He squinted as he looked up at me, shielding his eyes with his forearm, then addressed someone still hiding in the shadows, saying, "It's all right." From out of the darkness stepped a dozen frightened children.

"Any news?" the young man called to me. He spoke with a strange accent.

"What?" I asked.

"News?" he repeated.

"Wait there," I said, motioning with both hands. The children exchanged nervous looks as I crossed to the far side of the bridge and slid down the steep embankment. The littlest ones retreated to the shadows.

"Don't be afraid," I called. But only the young man remained in the light. "What are you doing here?" I asked.

"Waiting. Have you brought any news?" His looks and clothes were foreign.

"What do you mean?"

"Is it safe?" he pressed. "In town?" He wore a long black coat over a collarless white shirt.

"Of course it's safe," I laughed.

"He doesn't understand," a voice said from the shadows. It was the tall girl I had seen the first day. She sat in the dust, leaning against the cold stones of the bridge, the baby asleep in her lap. The twin boys stood beside her, barefoot. "Who are you?" she asked me.

I pointed in the direction of the farm. "Monsieur Hoirie's grandson."

A smile of relief spread across the young man's face. "We owe your grandfather a great deal. He has helped many."

"Where are you from?" I asked the girl, stepping into the shade. Her eyes seemed to glow in the darkness. The air was so cold it made me shiver.

"From everywhere," the young man answered, removing his glasses from around his ears and polishing them with a dirty handkerchief. His elbows poked through the torn sleeves of his coat.

"How come I never saw you before?" I asked.

"It's not safe for us to be seen," he answered.

"Why not?"

"Our parents are in hiding, and we must hide too."

"I don't understand," I said.

He shook his head sadly and replaced the glasses on his nose. "It's the way of the world." Then his voice brightened and he turned toward the children. "But soon it will be safe for us to go home."

"Why can't you go now?"

"They'll send for us when it's time."

"Isaac," the tall girl interrupted. "I think it's coming."

The young man turned his head to listen. The others froze. Still clutching the heavy book under one arm, he climbed the steep embankment to the bridge and peered down the dark, empty tunnel created by the overhanging branches. From below, the children fixed their eyes upon him, scarcely breathing until he signaled with a barely perceptible nod of the head. In an instant they scattered, vanishing among the trees.

"What is it?" I asked, climbing up beside him and looking along the pine path. I heard nothing but the murmur of water.

"The train," he said, walking back into the undergrowth. "Come with us. We'll hide you."

"What train?" I asked, looking once more down the empty right-of-way. "There aren't even any tracks." I turned back toward him, but he had disappeared.

C H A P T E R

Four

When I told Madame Jaboter of my encounter she grew pale, grabbed hold of my hands, and sat me down at the kitchen table.

"What did he look like, this young man?" she whispered.

I mentioned his glasses, the long coat torn at the elbows, his sparse brown beard.

"Did he tell you his name?" she asked nervously. I shook my head. "Are you sure?"

And then I remembered the girl had called him Isaac.

"Oh my God!" Madame Jaboter moaned.

"What's wrong?" I asked.

"Etienne, Etienne!" She dropped my hands and clutched at her apron. "What were they doing?"

"Hiding, I think. They were under the bridge reciting something, like a school lesson."

"From a big book?" she asked, staring past me into the sitting room.

"Yes," I replied. "How did you know?"

"Like those?" She pointed toward the shelf of tall books beside the fireplace.

"About that size, I guess, but all ragged and torn," I replied, beginning to feel her fear.

Madame Jaboter stood up and circled the kitchen, muttering, "My God, my God!" her hands pressed to her temples. "And the other children, what did they look like?" she asked.

"I didn't really get a good look at them, except for the four I'd seen before."

"You saw these children another time?" she asked, leaning on the table, her face close to mine. "When? Where?"

I told her of the day I arrived in Mont Brulant and described the tall girl carrying the baby.

"Sarah," she murmured.

"Who's that?" I asked.

Madame Jaboter pursed her lips and shook her head.

"Do you know them?" I asked again. "Who are they?" But she wouldn't answer. So I told her to wait there and ran upstairs to retrieve the small gold bracelet. "I found this near the old bridge," I said, laying it on the table. She picked it up in her thick red fingers and spread it across the deep creases of her palm, tears filling her yellow eyes.

"Why did you have to go there?" she said mournfully.

"Is it Sarah's?" I asked.

She shook her head. "It was the baby's." Then she buried her face in her hands and began to sob.

"I'll return it to her," I said, trying to understand her tears.

"It's too late," she cried.

"I'll find them again."

"No!" she shouted, startling me. "Don't go back. Etienne, please, promise me."

"Why not?"

"They're not real, they're ghosts," she whispered.

"No they're not," I scoffed. "I saw them. They talked to me."

"Etienne, those children died years ago."

Grand-père limped into the kitchen and dropped a stack of newly repaired books on the table. Madame Jaboter closed her hand but not before Grand-père spotted the bracelet.

"Are you filling the boy's head with your superstitious nonsense again?" he asked, his face dark with anger.

"But he saw them. They spoke to him."

"Enough!" he cried, taking my arm and pulling me out of the kitchen. "What's done is done."

"You can't will them away!" she shouted, standing in the doorway. "They won't be forgotten. They want their revenge."

Grand-père set his jaw and kept walking, yanking my arm with each limping step.

"Who are they?" I asked, trying to free myself.

"*They?*" he snapped, releasing my arm and throwing open the orchard gate. "They're nothing but the bad dreams of a guilty conscience." Inside among the trees he grew calmer, walking the long rows, inspecting the ripening fruit. Finally he lowered himself onto the matted grass. "Sit," he said, patting the ground beside him. He pulled a pear from a low branch, removed the folding knife from his pocket, and sliced it open. "Another month and they'll be ready to ship," he observed, cutting me a small piece. The meat was white, stone hard, and very sour.

He watched a single white cloud float across the blistering sky, then said absently, "War is terrible, especially for children. They always suffer the most." He spoke not to me, it seemed, but to the trees. "During the last war thousands of children passed through Mont Brulant, thousands! Most of them came alone, sent on ahead by their parents in a desperate rush to save them from the bombs and the guns. Week after week, month after month they arrived, exhausted, hungry, afraid. Some mornings I found them asleep right here among the trees, their pockets filled with unripe pears. They were starving."

"What did you do?" I asked, wondering if he ignored them like the children by the side of the road or shooed them away for stealing.

"What could I do? What could any of us really do? It was like trying to hold back a flood with your fingers. We tried to help them, the whole town did. But there were too many. They slept in

the barn, the attic, under the trees. Some stayed a few days, others a few weeks. In the middle of the night they would vanish, but by the next morning new ones had taken their place."

He paused again, then looked directly at me. "We had our own safety to consider too, our own children...your mother."

A cold, hard light filled his eyes. "The harvest that year was a bad one. Most of the farms were empty. All the young men were off fighting or in hiding. There wasn't enough food. Those were terrible times, times I'd rather forget."

"What happened to all the children? Where did they go?"

"Who knows." He shrugged, his voice a mixture of regret and annoyance. "Some tried to escape over the ocean, others went farther south. By the time I learned their names they were gone."

"Do you remember one called Sarah?" I asked.

He shrugged.

"Or Isaac?"

"They were all named Sarah and Isaac," he said. Then more softly he muttered again, "What's done is done." But from the troubled look in his eyes it didn't seem done at all.

And I thought, if I can find Isaac and Sarah and bring them back to the farm, then maybe Grand-père and Madame Jaboter will stop feeling so bad about them. So, whenever it was too hot to do anything else, I rode slowly back to the bridge, searching the shadows, listening for voices. Sometimes, when the wind was up, I heard their distant chanting. But, though I called their names, they never answered. Still, I found more evidence that they had been there: a pair of old-fashioned rimless glasses like the ones Isaac wore, a cracked wristwatch, the hands frozen at five minutes to twelve, a single infant shoe worn through at the sole, three marbles, a handful of tarnished copper coins, two bent keys, a blackened silver necklace, and, my favorite, an enameled pocketknife with two rusty blades. I kept them in a shoe box, and every night after dinner, while Grand-père read, I cleaned and polished them, especially the knife. From time to time Grand-père would look across at me, his face slack, his eyes vacant, lost in thought. Then he would shake his head slightly, as if to rid himself of some annoying ache, shut his eyes a moment, and return to his book. I took care to keep my collection a secret from Madame Jaboter.

C H A P T E R
Five

As the pears began to ripen, Grand-père and I set about harvesting them, climbing ladders into the uppermost branches, filling the white sacks that hung across our chests until the straps cut our shoulders. We emptied the pears into wooden crates and delivered them to the depot every three or four days for shipment to the city. The work was hard, the days long and hot. Mosquitoes and bees swarmed around us as we gathered the fruit. My neck and shoulders ached from the heavy sack, the soles of my feet from balancing on the ladder rungs, my arms from reaching and pulling and reaching and pulling twelve hours a day.

Grand-père was so anxious to harvest the orchard quickly, before the pears became too soft to ship, that one night we picked them by the faint silver light of the full moon. We worked in silence, casting eerie gray shadows on the colorless grass. When I paused to look out over the darkened farmhouse and the silver fields, Grand-père whispered, "How much we miss by sleeping this time away." It was both beautiful and sad. The countryside seemed empty of everyone but us, as though we were the last surviving inhabitants of Mont Brulant.

As I finished the crown of one tree and began to climb down, the sound of a distant train whistle floated over the warm, still air. It came not from the direction of town but from the woods below Mont Brulant. I turned my head from side to side, wondering if it was an echo or some trick of the wind, but the night was completely windless.

"Grand-père," I whispered, "what is that?"

"What is what?" he asked, looking up from the crate he was packing.

"The train."

He turned his ear toward town, then held his watch up to the moonlight. "Not due for another hour."

"It didn't come from town, but from over there," I said, pointing toward the shadowy black mass of Mont Brulant.

He followed my hand and frowned. "Couldn't be. You must have dozed off."

"I'm not tired," I said.

"It's late," he insisted. "Come, enough pears for one day. The rest can wait."

I held the heavy sack away from the ladder and had begun to climb down when the sound returned, louder this time, and

not only a train whistle but the rhythmic clanking of freight cars. I peered through the black branches of the pear tree, searching for a distant wisp of smoke.

"Grand-père," I whispered, handing him my sack. "There it is again."

This time he didn't even turn his head. "The night deceives," he replied, "especially under a full moon."

"Can't you hear it?" I asked.

"Etienne, enough!" he snapped, deep creases furrowing his forehead. "There's no train in that direction for fifty miles."

"But I hear it."

"And those who hold a conch shell to their ear swear they hear the sea. To bed with you. It's late." He hammered the last crate shut, then led me slowly out through the orchard gate.

Later that night I awoke to the sound of something scraping against the house. "Grand-père?" I whispered nervously. The noise stopped a moment, then resumed. I lay still. No, it wasn't against the side of the house, I realized, but out in the barnyard. The children, I thought, jumping from bed. They're stealing pears.

I looked toward the orchard. The moon hung large and yellow above the trees, casting a pale gray shadow beyond Reveuse. She had escaped from her stall and was trying to open one of the pear crates near the gate, gnawing the soft wood slats with her teeth.

"Reveuse," I whispered, "leave that alone." She glanced up at me, then continued to chew on the wood.

I dressed quickly and slipped out of the house, intending to return her to the barn. But as I took hold of her halter the sound of the train whistle returned, drifting through the moonlit air like the sorrowful cry of mourning doves. Reveuse turned toward Mont Brulant and seemed to prick up her ears.

"Grand-père's wrong, isn't he?" I whispered to her. "There *is* a train over there. You hear it, don't you?" Reveuse snorted once and dropped her head.

I tiptoed to the house and peered in through the window. Grand-père lay asleep on the couch, a book across his chest, orange embers glowing faintly in the grate. I hurried back across the shadowy yard and quietly saddled up Reveuse, then led her around the barn and out to the road.

"Where is it? Can you show me?" I asked, climbing onto her back. She set off with unusual determination, almost trotting toward the great black mountain. I leaned forward, tightly clutching her neck, breathing in the warm, musty smell of her white coat. In the darkness every stone and tree seemed vaguely menacing. Night creatures scurried into the shadows as we passed, their sudden movements startling me. Halfway to the mountain Reveuse slowed, then stopped. "Let's go back," I whispered. "We'll return tomorrow, in daylight. I can't see anything anyway."

Reveuse sniffed the air, snorted again, then without my prodding continued on in the same direction. It grew darker as the moon dropped behind the trees. The pine forest at the foot of Mont Brulant rose up before us, as dense and impenetrable as a prison wall. The road ended. We crossed open pasture, looking for the opening in the trees. "There's nothing here," I whispered, trying not to hear any more train whistles, ready to believe it was as Grand-père said, just a dream. "Let's go home." But Reveuse trotted on, yanking her head indignantly whenever I tried to turn her back.

And then the trees seemed to open up, revealing their long, dark tunnel to nowhere. Everything was just as before: no rails, no train, no smell of smoke, just pine needles. Reveuse stepped more cautiously, her reluctance returning. I could feel her heartbeat quicken.

"Please, Reveuse," I pleaded, my eyes unable to pierce the darkness. "I don't like this." But she walked on until a pale gray object loomed up before us. "Go back," I whispered in terror, yanking on her reins. This time she stopped. We had reached the stone bridge.

"Why'd you come here?" I asked into her ear. "There's no train. Let's go home." But she wouldn't budge. I dismounted and tried to turn her around. With a sudden jerk of her head she sent me tumbling down the steep embankment toward the stream. "Reveuse!" I cried, scrambling up the loose and shifting soil in a panic, afraid she would bolt for the farm, leaving me there alone. My feet slipped and I fell to my knees. I grabbed at the earth, feeling something hard between my fingers, and shook my hand away in terror, then looked down and discovered an old pen lying among the pine needles. Slipping it in my pocket, I hurried up to Reveuse, jumped on her back, and turned toward home. It wasn't until the woods were far behind us that I began to breathe more easily. Then I took out the pen and uncapped it. It was not tarnished like all the other things I had found. The gold nib shone brightly, even under a moonless sky. And when I drew it across my forearm, a thick line of ink stained my skin blue. In the darkness it looked like the numbers I had seen on the arms of begging refugee children.

The sun was just coming over the horizon when we reached the farm. Grand-père stood at the stove frying thick slabs of ham, his sleeves rolled above his elbows, the fine white hair at the back of his head tinged pink by the early morning light.

"You're out early," he called, showing none of the anger I had expected.

"Just to the woods," I answered with relief, tying up Reveuse and washing beneath the pump. I scrubbed my ink-stained forearm, then rubbed it dry with a rough towel, but the blue line remained.

"What did you find this time?" Grand-père asked, setting the eggs on the table.

I held up the pen. "It still works."

"I see," he said, taking hold of my wrist. His expression darkened as he studied the stain. Then he uncapped the pen and drew it across his open palm. Nothing came out. He shook it and tried again, but it was empty now and not only empty but tarnished. The gold point had turned black.

"Who did this to you?" he asked, his voice trembling.

"No one. I did."

"Not with this," he insisted, shaking it again. "It's dry as dust."

"But it wasn't before," I replied, confused and frightened. "It's just a little ink."

"Don't let Madame Jaboter see this," he whispered hoarsely.

"Why not?" I asked.

"Because this is what they did to the ones they made into slaves!"

"What do you mean?" I asked, alarmed.

"Nothing. I don't mean anything." Grand-père retreated, looking away. "This heat is making me as foolish as Madame Jaboter. Eat your breakfast. We've got work to do."

CHAPTER

Six

Grand-père's words continued to haunt me, but he would not explain what he meant. In the unbearable heat of the next few days he rarely spoke. That Thursday, as we drove Madame Jaboter back to town, waves of heat rose like steam from the bone-dry dirt. Reveuse clopped slowly along the familiar road while Grand-père and Madame Jaboter dozed. I sat in back among the pear crates, carving my name into the slats with my newly polished pocket-knife, occasionally leaning out over the side of the wagon to feel the faint breeze stirred by our sluggish pace.

As we came over a small rise what looked like a long line of children appeared in the shimmering distance. I stood upon one of the crates for a better view. Reveuse raised her head and slowed as if expecting to stop. The tall, spindly girl, Sarah, led the group. I shook Grand-père's shoulder and pointed to them, saying, "There they are."

He squinted a moment through one eye, then shut it heavily.

"So many new ones," he muttered, his chin resting on his chest. "Not enough food. Bad times, bad times."

But Madame Jaboter snapped instantly out of her reverie and asked, "What new ones?" peering forward into the haze. The wagon neared the ragged group, and I pointed to them, practically touching Sarah. She reached out to me, and as she did the sleeve of her shapeless dress slid back, revealing the stain of blue numbers across her forearm.

"What are you pointing at?" Madame Jaboter whispered, her eyes narrow with fear.

"Grand-père, stop the wagon!" I called.

"What's the matter?" he asked, startled awake.

Madame Jaboter took his arm. "Etienne sees something."

He called to Reveuse, "Whoa, my lady." The children began to disappear over the next rise. I leapt from the wagon and ran after them. But the faster I ran the faster they seemed to retreat, drifting out of reach like a desert mirage.

Grand-père cried, "Stop, Etienne! Where are you going? It's much too hot."

"He sees the children," Madame Jaboter cried. "Come back, Etienne!" Her shrill voice pierced the thick heat.

I stopped at the crest of a hill and watched the children shuffle off into the haze. Grand-père clucked at Reveuse to back up.

"Etienne, there's nothing there," he called.

"But he sees them," Madame Jaboter insisted.

"He sees nothing. The heat plays tricks. He was dreaming. We all were."

"He saw the children."

"Again with the children?" Grand-père snapped. "There are no children. For the last time, there are no children."

"And may God forgive us," Madame Jaboter muttered bitterly, tears spilling down her cheeks.

When we reached town Madame Jaboter came around to the back of the wagon and took my hands in hers, placing her tear-swollen face close to mine. "I know I'm just a silly old woman," she said, "but do this for me, please, Etienne. Do you promise?"

"Do what?" I asked.

"Promise first."

"Let the boy be," Grand-père scolded.

"Don't talk to them," Madame Jaboter begged.

"You only make him want to," Grand-père insisted, sitting hunched over, his eyes wrinkled with annoyance.

Then, for the first time, she noticed the ink stain on my forearm and began to moan. "Oh my God, my God! Did you see this?" She pressed my arm to her cheek.

"It's nothing," I insisted, trying to pull free, frightened by her terror. I looked to Grand-père for help.

"The boy was playing with a pen, that's all," he explained, his own voice suddenly tremulous with worry.

"But Monsieur Hoirie, the tattoo!" She held my arm out to him. "You can't deny this. It's a sign."

"This heat is making us all crazy," he replied. "The boy did it himself. Tell her."

"I found a pen," I explained.

"In the woods?" she asked.

"Of course in the woods," Grand-père growled. "He has a box full of such things. So what!"

Madame Jaboter covered her mouth with one hand, holding my wrist tightly with the other.

"He has nothing to fear," Grand-père continued. "That time is over and done with."

"What's over?" I asked, but neither seemed to hear me. I had become invisible to them.

"Maybe for us it's over," she said, "but not for the children. For them it will never be over."

"What are you talking about?" I cried.

"Nonsense!" he shouted. "What's done is done. It's finished. Now enough."

"How can you be so sure?" she asked, pushing my wrist toward him. "Look at that. It's not over. It will never be over. One by one they will take them all away, all the children, every last one of them, to punish us for abandoning them."

"Grand-père, answer me!" I shouted, wrenching my arm free. They looked at me in stunned silence, awakening to my presence. Across the empty square Monsieur Jaboter stepped from his shop and called to his wife.

"It's for your grandfather to explain," she said. Then, kissing my forehead, she whispered, "May God protect you," and hurried away, wiping her eyes on her apron.

"We'll talk," Grand-père promised, "but first we deliver our pears." He led Reveuse over to the town fountain, then to the depot, where we unloaded the heavy crates, Grand-père pausing frequently to wipe his sweating face. After checking the mail room, he climbed back into the wagon, his cheeks and forehead glistening. He clucked once at Reveuse, then turned toward me as we rolled slowly out of town.

"I had hoped to spare you this, to see you grow up in a world that didn't have to know about such things."

"What things?" I asked.

He shook his head wearily. "War is a terrible thing, a time of universal madness when men behave like beasts—worse than beasts, like demons. All wars are that way, but during the last one there was a special madness, a kind of killing we had never seen before. No one was safe, not old men or women, not children, not even babies. People were killed just for the sake of killing."

His eyes sought mine. "They would have taken you from your

mother had you been born—you who have done no one any harm—just because of who you are, of who your father is: a Jew. They took away so many Jews, all they could find, took them away and killed them. Don't ask me why. I don't know. Had your father not been in hiding they would have taken him too.

"Wars are supposed to be fought between soldiers. But this one was not. They slaughtered the innocents, pulled babies from their mothers' arms, children from their teachers. I didn't understand it then; I still don't. It was madness, the end of a God-fearing world."

He looked down at his spotted, calloused hands. "For a long time we thought the war would not touch us here. We threatened no one, wanted only to plant our crops. But then the children began to arrive, Jewish children. We tried to care for them, the whole town tried. It was hard, especially in winter, but we did what we could, turning the whole village into an almshouse. From every window and door terrified orphans peered out at us, trembling whenever news of the approaching enemy, the Nazis, reached us.

"The children kept coming, some by train, some on foot, some in wagons piled high with suitcases. It was as though all Europe had said, 'Send the children to Mont Brulant, they will be safe there.' And we thought they would be. What harm could they do such a powerful enemy? They wanted only what all children want, to live in peace.

"Your mother helped care for the smallest ones. Your grand-mother—God rest her soul—wore herself out cooking for them and sewing their tattered clothes."

Reveuse left the main road, pulling languidly uphill. "They used to sit on these walls, waiting for us," Grand-père recalled, pointing to the stones lining both sides of the road—the road where I had first spotted Sarah and the others. "They knew Reveuse by name. When we passed they would cry, 'Pears, Monsieur Reveuse, pears!' running alongside the wagon. It was the only word they knew in our language, that and *merci*.

"And then one terrible day in late summer the Nazis marched into town with tanks and machine guns and ordered us to deliver all the children into their hands. They said they would care for them, would feed and clothe and school them until they could be reunited with their parents. A few of us didn't believe them. We'd heard rumors, awful stories about terrible places called concentration camps where men, women, and children were treated like slaves and left to die of illness and starvation. But what could we do? If we didn't give them the children, they'd arrest us too or shoot us on the spot. I tell you, they weren't human."

"And you gave them the children?" I asked in disbelief, staring at the empty stone walls.

"I wish to God we hadn't," Grand-père slowly admitted. "But there are no easy choices in wartime, only agonizing, heartbreaking ones."

"Would you have let them take me?" I asked, trembling.

"Oh, Etienne," he said, moaning, "you are my flesh and blood. They were foreigners, strangers."

The stain on my arm began to burn. I rubbed it with my open palm. "But they were just boys and girls like me, Grand-père, and babies. You said so yourself. I've seen some of them. They're still hiding."

"No, Etienne, they're gone, all of them. I watched them go. As long as I live I will never forget that night." He shuddered and shook his head. "The Nazis ordered us to bring them all to the stone bridge below Mont Brulant. They said a special train would be waiting there. Any foreign children found after that train departed would be shot, along with the families hiding them. Shot! They would shoot the children and they would shoot us too, for protecting them. That's the kind of madness I mean, a madness that turns right into wrong and wrong into right. In such a world everyone is guilty."

"Why didn't you all just run away?" I asked, bringing my forearm up to my mouth.

"Run where? There was no place to hide. The Nazis were everywhere. They would have hunted us down and shot us like squirrels— What's wrong with your arm?"

"It burns," I cried, tears rushing to my eyes.

He took it in his hands. It was red and chafed from rubbing. "We'll get you some water," he said, his face full of alarm, and

called to Reveuse to hurry home, snapping the reins across her back. When we reached the barnyard I leapt from the wagon and buried my arm in Reveuse's trough. The scorching pain slowly eased until it was a dull ache that left my whole arm limp.

I ate dinner that night lying on the couch feeling slightly feverish, my wrist wrapped in a damp cloth. Grand-père sat beside me, holding my plate while I raised one forkful at a time to my mouth. He looked tired and worried.

"I'm better," I said, forcing my lips into a smile.

"Does it still burn?" he asked.

I shook my head.

"Let's see." He lifted my arm and carefully unwrapped the bandage. The skin was white and wrinkled from the wetness, and the blue stain had begun to fade.

"Does that hurt?" he asked, pressing lightly.

"No, it's better."

He lay my arm down.

"Did Isaac leave those books?" I asked, pointing to the bookshelves.

He looked at me with surprise. "How did you know his name?"

"Madame Jaboter."

"Of course," he replied with relief.

"Who was he?"

"You should rest. We'll talk more tomorrow."

"Was he a teacher?" I asked.

"You're as stubborn as Madame Jaboter." He snorted. "Yes, I think he was. He came here with a schoolroom full of children. They worshiped him. More than that, they trusted him. He was very learned for such a young man, one of the few who could speak our language."

"I spoke to him," I said.

"That's not possible."

"He was holding a book just like those." I pointed toward the shelf with my chin.

Grand-père studied the volumes a moment. "Believe me," he said sadly, "it wasn't Isaac. It couldn't have been."

"But he—"

Grand-père put his hand on my shoulder to silence me. "Listen a moment, *mon cher*, then decide." His voice was full of regret. "Your grandmother and I were very attached to him. He was like a son to us." His eyes grew moist. "He stayed here most of that awful summer, slept in the hayloft with the children, took care of them like a father. And every morning after breakfast, no matter what, he conducted classes in the orchard, reading from those books, the children repeating his words, asking questions." He looked over his shoulder again at the shelf.

"There was a young girl too, no older than you are, but the war had made her very wise. She mothered all the little ones, comforted them in the dark, found them food. She was always holding an infant in those skinny little arms of hers. It used to break your grand-mère's heart to see her carrying the babies around."

"Sarah?" I asked.

"Yes, Sarah," he said, both startled and annoyed. "If Madame Jaboter has already told you all this, why ask me?"

"She only told me her name."

"Does it hurt?" he suddenly asked.

Without realizing it I had begun to rub my arm. "It's okay," I assured him. The skin tingled as feeling slowly returned. "Tell me about Sarah. Why didn't she leave with the others?"

"But she did," Grand-père insisted. "They all did, they had to. Soldiers were everywhere, banging on doors, poking their blood-stained bayonets into haystacks and mattresses. They knew all our hiding places. Resistance was impossible. It would only have caused more bloodshed. The night they ordered all the children out, the town was ringed by tanks. Where could we go?"

Grand-père rose and walked to the books, standing with his back to me. "So we gave up the children," he continued, almost in a whisper, "thousands of them. From every farmhouse and barn they came, holding hands, eyes bright with hope and terror. We told them they were going to meet their parents. The youngest ones believed us, but not Sarah. She knew. Still, she did her best to cheer the others.

"When we reached the bridge, the train was waiting for them, surrounded by flaming torches and soldiers with machine guns and snarling dogs. It wasn't the passenger train the Nazis had promised, it was for cattle! Whatever shred of hope we still clung to vanished in that moment as the soldiers rolled back the huge doors and ordered the children into the train. Shots were fired; the dogs growled and snapped; the children screamed, dropped their bundles, lost their shoes, their toys, even their bracelets and pens and pocketknives. Those who tried to run away were quickly recaptured and thrown into the cattle cars.

"Isaac could have saved himself. The train was meant for children only. But he insisted on staying with them. 'If I abandon them, I abandon myself,' he said as the boxcars filled. He was not concerned for his own safety. He wanted only to ease their suffering. They had no one else to turn to, no one they could trust. Somehow he alone, in the midst of all the madness, had not forgotten the difference between right and wrong."

Grand-père turned to face me, his face wrinkled with pain. "I think about those poor children every day. They're always with me. I see their frightened eyes, hear their screams. I can't sleep nights thinking how we led them to slaughter, not just us, the whole world, abandoning them in the middle of the night. It's a terrible thing to live with cowardice. Sometimes I think it's better not to live at all."

"But some of them escaped," I said. "I saw them under the bridge."

"If only they had." He took down one of the books and

touched his forehead to it. "Why don't the heavens crack? What have we become that such dreadful things are possible?"

His shoulders rose and fell in silent sobs. What he said next he spoke into the book. "Just before they slid the doors shut, Isaac shouted to me over the crying children and barking dogs: 'The law will one day bear fruit.' I didn't understand what he meant. 'Preserve it, please, for those who come after us.' The heavy door slammed shut and the world came to an end. I never saw him again, never saw any of them. It wasn't until a year later, while root feeding the pear trees, that I discovered what he meant. He had buried all his books in the orchard. I dug them up and restored them, one by one. It took me almost ten years. If Isaac were still alive, he would have come for them by now. He cherished them. They were his life."

Grand-père placed the book back on the shelf and sat next to me. "I haven't been back to the woods since that horrible night. Neither had Reveuse until this summer."

"That's why she won't cross that bridge," I declared.

"Perhaps. Reveuse forgets nothing. She and I share the same thoughts, only her conscience is clear. She didn't want to take Isaac and Sarah and the others there that night, I made her. The day after we gave up the children she broke my leg. I walked into her stall and she kicked me."

"You should have listened to her," I said indignantly.

"I wish I had," he murmured. "Better to have died with them

than to live with such guilt." He dropped heavily into his chair. "Those things you found, your box of treasures, they belonged to them."

"I thought so," I said, convinced now that the children were still hiding in the woods, perhaps even leaving those things for me to find.

"No one from the village has been back there since they pulled up the tracks."

"Why'd they do that?"

"Senseless defiance, I guess, like raising your fist to a bully after he's turned his back, or shutting the barn door after all the animals have escaped. We had to do something to keep from going mad."

"You weren't trying to hide what had happened?" I asked, sitting up.

Grand-père looked as if I'd slapped him across the face. "Hide? Hide from whom? Everyone here knew." He kneaded his face with his thick fingers. "Maybe you're right, maybe we thought we could hide the truth from ourselves, remove all the evidence, then gradually forget. But nothing can ease such a guilty conscience." Grand-père's voice grew slower, heavier. "We committed a terrible crime. If the Nazis had known we would protect the children with our lives, if they thought we would fight to keep them, they would not have taken them away, at least not so easily. They too would have had to pay a price." He looked down at his hands with disgust and said no more. A great chasm opened between us. I stood on one side of a deep, unbridgeable silence, Grand-père on the other.

Later that night, after Grand-père fell asleep, I walked up into the orchard and sat on the windless hill watching the fireflies dance, the pain in my arm nearly gone. What would I have done in his place? I wondered. How brave would *I* have been facing an entire army? I certainly wouldn't have given up the children without a fight, I thought. The whole town should have risen up in arms, like Grand-père said. Why hadn't they? But then I remembered how frightened I'd been in the woods the night I found the pen, how every shadow and shuddering leaf had made me tremble. Who was I to talk of bravery? But I'm just a boy, I concluded, and Grand-père is a man. He should have protected them.

Still, they hadn't all died. I was certain some had escaped. I'd seen them, heard their chanting, even talked with them. Isaac hadn't meant to lead them into slavery but to help them escape and hide. Somehow they'd managed to flee and return to Mont Brulant, where they were still awaiting word that the war was over, that it was safe to come out. But no one knew they were there, no one but me.

CHAPTER
Seven

*T*hat same night, after making sure Grand-père was sound asleep, I saddled up Reveuse and left the farm. This time I would not be intimidated by the night, I told myself. There was nothing to fear. The waist-high wheat shimmered under the liquid light of the full moon. Neighboring farmhouses stood like great granite blocks, casting gray shadows across silver barnyards. A toothless old dog barked once as we passed, then fell silent. Nothing looked or felt familiar. Even Reveuse seemed transformed, breaking into a spirited gallop, as eager as I to reach the woods. And when we got there she did not resist my urgings but approached the bridge and then, for the first time, crossed it. The air felt as it does before a powerful thunderstorm, thick and moist, full of explosive energy, as though the forest itself were holding its breath, waiting anxiously for something overwhelming to occur.

I pulled back on the reins, stopping Reveuse in the middle of the darkened path. Nothing stirred. Not even moonlight penetrated the thick canopy of trees. In a trembling whisper I called,

"Isaac? Sarah? You can come out now. It's safe. No one will hurt you." I turned my head to listen, then called more loudly, "Don't be afraid."

And then the trees began to shiver with the wind of small voices, hundreds of them, distant murmurings punctuated by tiny dots of light. Reveuse shivered too, her powerful shoulder muscles twitching beneath her thick white coat. "Easy, girl," I whispered, patting her neck, my own arms and legs quivering. The lights grew brighter, the voices louder. From every direction, down the mountain, up from the river, along the edge of the old right-of-way, children approached, clutching lighted candles. Some chewed on bread, others on pears. They clung to bits of cloth, to ragged dolls, to each other's hands. The oldest cradled babies.

I recognized Sarah as she approached with an infant in her arms, followed by the twins. I was relieved to see them. "You can go home now," I said, slipping from Reveuse's back. "The war's over. You don't need to hide anymore."

But she didn't answer. None of them did.

"Where's Isaac?" I called after her as more children emerged from the shadows. I walked among them, telling them they had nothing to fear, but they seemed not to hear or understand me.

Then Isaac appeared, standing by the bridge surrounded by small children, a large book under one arm, his free hand patting their heads and shoulders, comforting them. "Everything's going to be all right," he insisted, "just stay together." A few children whimpered. "Don't be frightened," he whispered. "I'm not going to leave you."

I hurried forward to tell him they were free to return home, but before I could, Isaac held up his hand to silence everyone, then looked down the dark tunnel and cocked his head slightly.

"They're coming!" he declared. "Don't be frightened. They won't hurt us." The youngest began to sob.

At the end of the long black tunnel a single dot of yellow light appeared. I turned to Isaac and asked, "What's that?"

"Our train."

"There is no train," I said, watching in disbelief as the light grew larger. "The war's over."

"Yes, for us it is," he said flatly. "We're going home."

"That's not a train; it must be the moon," I said.

He smiled and shook his head.

"Then it must be some kind of reflection. There aren't any tracks here." I kicked through the pine needles to show him, but as I did he took hold of my arm and pulled me from the path. The ground began to tremble.

"Is everyone here?" he shouted, counting heads.

"Come back to the farm with me," I told them.

"You've already done too much," he said, walking among the children, trying to calm them. "We don't want to endanger your family further. Perhaps one day, when all this is over."

The sound of a train whistle pierced the night air. "Grand-

père," I blurted out. "The train!" I stepped back onto the path and tripped over wooden ties and steel rails vibrating with the motion of wheels.

"What is that?" I shouted, pointing toward an enormous light.

"Our destiny," Isaac shouted over the noise of the approaching engine.

"But it can't be."

"You see for yourself."

A huge black locomotive loomed up behind the blinding beam of light. Beyond it boxcars, dozens of them, stretched off into the darkness.

"I don't understand," I shouted, trembling. "What's happening?"

The brakes began to squeal. The children covered their ears. The locomotive rumbled past, coming to an abrupt stop just beyond the bridge.

"I'm here," Isaac assured them. "We're going to be all right. Just stay together." He moved quickly among them, wiping their eyes, holding their hands.

And then, as if on command, the huge doors slid open and hundreds of armed soldiers jumped down, shouting, "In! Now!" Children pushed past me, eyes aflame with terror. Soldiers prodded them with rifles and barking dogs. I hid behind a tree, watching, too petrified to move.

Then someone took hold of my arm and I screamed. It was

Isaac. "Don't be frightened," he said. "They don't want you."

"But the war's over," I cried.

"Not for us," he said, sadly. "We don't have much time. Tell Monsieur Hoirie we will never forget his kindness."

"Don't go, it's a trick."

"We must. If they find any of us after the train departs they will burn the town."

"Hurry!" someone shouted. The train sounded its whistle. A huge plume of black smoke shot into the air. The boxcars jolted forward, throwing screaming children against each other. Isaac handed me the large book he carried. "Keep this," he said. "Treasure it." Then he climbed up into the already rolling boxcar, joining the hundreds of gleaming, hollow eyes that stared out at me through the darkness. "Remember what you saw here," he cried as the train carried him off.

I awoke the next morning on a bed of pine needles as the first rays of sunlight turned the forest floor orange. Reveuse stood beside me, prodding my legs with her muzzle. I sat up and rubbed the sleep from my eyes, wondering what time it was. Grand-père would be worried. Then I remembered the previous night and jumped to my feet, looking for signs of the train, the children, the soldiers. But there were none: The tracks were gone; the forest was as empty and peaceful as it had been all summer.

I mounted Reveuse and rode back to the farm. Dew sparkled

on the second growth of hay. The heat had finally broken. Along the road Grand-père's few remaining neighbors were already out scything the fields. The old bent men waved to me as I passed.

"I was beginning to wonder what had become of you," Grand-père said as I entered the barnyard. He was scattering feed for the chickens. "Your breakfast is on the table. We have much to do today."

"I fell asleep in the woods," I said, relieved he was not angry.

"That's what summer evenings are for," he replied, taking the reins from my hands and leading Reveuse over to the trough. "How's your arm this morning?"

I rolled up my sleeve and squinted in the bright morning light. "Grand-père, look!" I said, holding it up. The stain was gone.

CHAPTER

Eight

W e finished harvesting the pears that week, picked the corn, cut the wheat and alfalfa, then shipped two dozen hens to market. As the end of my vacation drew near the weather turned sharply colder and the linden trees began to yellow. Once more after dinner a fire blazed in the grate; I slept under a heavy quilt. Grand-père spoke little during those final days, getting ready, he said, for the long silence of winter. But it seemed to me that the memory of the children gave him no rest. One morning I found him wandering through the empty orchard mumbling to himself. Another time he stood alone in the barn, staring off into space. When I asked what he was thinking, he muttered, "What might have been."

Late one night, a sharp wind threw the shutters against the house, waking me. I tiptoed halfway down the stairs and found Grand-père sitting motionless before the fire, one of the large books open across his lap. For one terrible moment I thought he had stopped breathing, but then he sighed, his shoulders rising slowly, then dropping heavily, sadly.

"Grand-père, are you all right?" I whispered.

He turned, his hollow gray eyes searching the dark hall. "What are you doing up so late, *mon cher*?" he asked.

"The wind woke me. Can't you sleep?"

"Old men don't need much sleep," he replied. "Go back to bed."

"Can I sit by the fire a minute? It's cold upstairs."

He motioned me toward him, closing the book and removing his bad leg from the footstool before the grate. I sat on the cushion and drew my feet under me, watching the small orange flames glide along the remaining log. I wanted our last days together to be as happy as our first; I wanted to see Grand-père smile again. But everything seemed to have changed since our talk. The farm itself felt different. The orchard was bare, the fields harvested. Where before the morning light itself seemed filled with excitement, it now seemed dusty and dull. It was time for summer to end. In spirit it had already fled.

"Why don't you come and live with us this winter?" I asked, feeling the fire's warmth on my hands and face.

"I can't," he said listlessly.

"Why not?"

"Who'd take care of Reveuse, or the chickens…or repair the books?" He glanced up at the high shelf. "Someone has to be here if he returns."

"But you said—"

"I know. Just a foolish old man's last hope."

I watched the firelight dance across his vacant eyes. "They all died, didn't they?" I asked. The reflected flames seemed to flutter a moment, to burn more brightly, then subside.

"Yes, they all died," Grand-père lamented, nodding slowly. "No one tried to save them, no one…no one." His voice trailed off and his eyes shut.

My last day on the farm I took Reveuse out for a long ride just before sunset. Most of the fields were stubble now, the lush green of summer giving way to a dormant brown, the blue sky a smoky white. In the woods the pine trees had begun to shed their needles, dropping them noiselessly to the forest floor, providing a fresh carpet of bright orange and ocher.

I saw it all differently now. In the absolute stillness I heard the shouting soldiers, the sobbing children, the terrifying roar of the locomotive. For the last time I dismounted and walked along the path, my feet kicking up showers of needles. They had tried to forget, Grand-père and the others, the old people of Mont Brulant, but the children would not be forgotten; what happened in those woods could never be forgotten. Madame Jaboter was right—the souls of a thousand lost children haunted the place. I could feel them now, clinging to my arms, whispering in my ears, begging to be remembered. And I promised them I would remember, always.

•   •   •   •   •

That summer was my last on the farm. When Grand-père kissed my cheeks at the depot and said good-bye, I felt I would never see him again. He looked frail and troubled standing beside the tracks, waving listlessly as the train pulled away. That winter he took sick, developed pneumonia, and, according to Madame Jaboter's last letter, began hearing voices. One bitterly cold night he wandered out into the orchard. She found him there the next morning. We buried him in the small cemetery at the edge of Mont Brulant almost exactly a year after Grand-mère died.

As Grand-père had predicted, no one wanted to buy the farm, so we sold what we could of the furniture and farm implements, then boarded up the old house and found a home for Reveuse closer to town. I kept only two things of Grand-père's, his pipe and the shelf of books he had so lovingly restored. Eventually I learned to read the ancient Hebrew contained within them and grew as attached to their wise counsel, their numerous laws concerning right and wrong, as Isaac had been. Grand-père, may he rest in peace, had not been able to save the children, but he had preserved the books of the law, the great Talmud, which had sustained Jewish life for two thousand years. I know now that all too few during that terrible war had proved braver, that most had sacrificed the stranger for their own safety, then tried to forget what they had done. But the dead would not be forgotten, they would not be forgotten.

ABOUT THE AUTHOR

Steven Schnur is the author of several books for children, including *Hannah and Cyclops* (Bantam), as well as collections of essays for adults. Mr. Schnur, who teaches literature and creative writing at Sarah Lawrence College, lives in Scarsdale, New York.

ABOUT THE ILLUSTRATOR

Herbert Tauss is an internationally known artist whose work has been awarded gold, silver, and bronze medals from the Society of Illustrators. He has illustrated limited-edition classics published by the Franklin Library. An instructor at the Fashion Institute of Technology and at Syracuse University's master's program, Mr. Tauss lives in Garrison, New York.